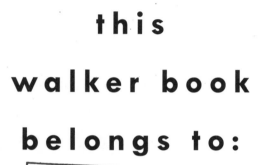

## this
## walker book
## belongs to:

---------------------

---------------------

---------------------

(a birthday something)
for neal – J.F.

**To all children on their birthdays
– C.R.**

First published in the UK 2018 by Walker Books Ltd
87 Vauxhall Walk, London SE11 5HJ

This edition published 2019

First published in the USA 2017 by Roaring Brook Press,
a division of Holtzbrink Publishing Holdings Limited Partnership

1 3 5 7 9 10 8 6 4 2

Text © 2017 by Julie Fogliano

Illustrations © 2017 by Christian Robinson

The right of Julie Fogliano and Christian Robinson to be identified as the author and illustrator
respectively of this work has been asserted by them in accordance with the Copyright,
Designs and Patents Act 1988

Printed in China

British Library Cataloguing in Publication Data: a catalogue record
for this book is available from the British Library

ISBN 978-1-4063-8639-4

www.walker.co.uk

# when's my birthday?

Julie Fogliano Christian Robinson

WALKER BOOKS
AND SUBSIDIARIES
LONDON · BOSTON · SYDNEY · AUCKLAND

when's my birthday?
where's my birthday?
how many days until
my birthday?

will my birthday be on tuesday?
will my birthday be tomorrow?
will my birthday be in winter?

will my birthday be in spring?

will my birthday have some singing?
will we sing so happy happy?
will we dance around and round?
will we jump and jump and jump?

ny days until
nday?

i'd like a pony
for my birthday
and a necklace
for my birthday.

i'd like a
chicken for
my birthday.

i'd like a ball
to bounce
and bounce.

i'd like a big cake on my birthday
with lots of chocolate on my birthday
and lots of candles on my birthday
1, 2, 3, 4, 5, and 6!

i'd like some wishes on my birthday.
i'd like some kisses on my birthday.
i'd like some berries on my birthday
and tiny sandwiches with soup.

and you're invited
to my birthday.

and she's invited
to my birthday.

and he's invited
to my birthday.

and you and
you and you.

and you can wear your fancy dresses
or you can wear your fuzzy slippers
or you can wear a hat with feathers
or a helmet with a cape.

if it ever is my birthday...
will it never be my birthday?
is it almost happy birthday?
happy happy day to me!

when's my birthday?
where's my birthday?
how many days until
my birthday?

in the morning it's my birthday!
i'm not sleeping till my birthday.
i'm just waiting till my birthday.
i'm just yawning till my birthday.
i'm just dreaming of my bluuuurfday.
happy snore and snore to me!

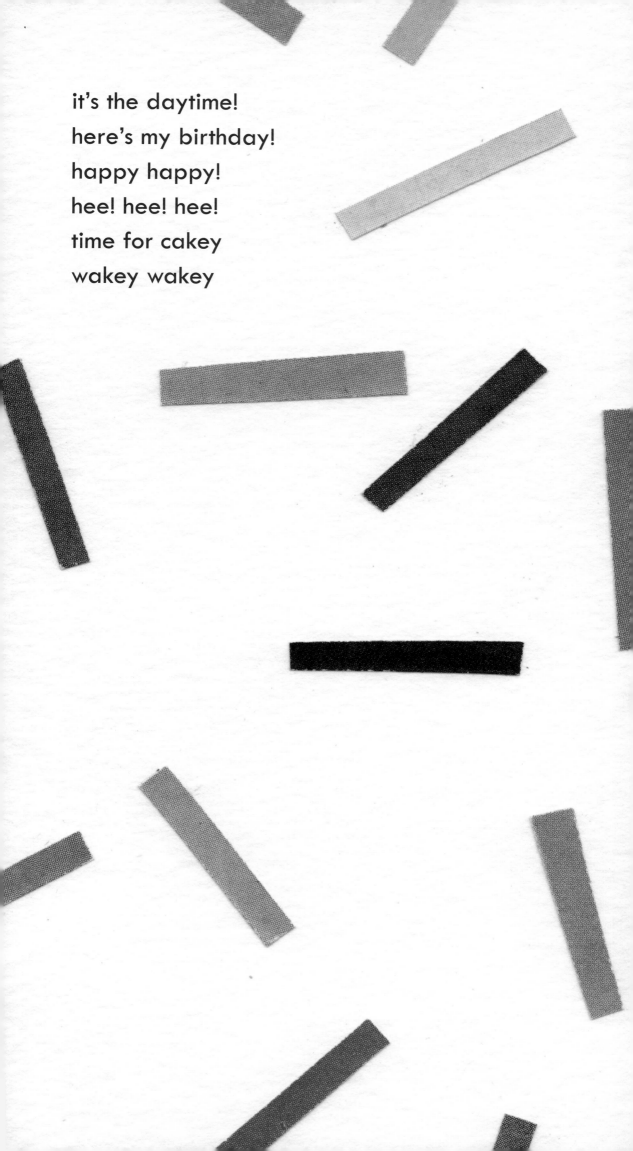

it's the daytime!
here's my birthday!
happy happy!
hee! hee! hee!
time for cakey
wakey wakey

happy happy day to me!

# When's Your Birthday?

January 1 2 3 4

February

March 8 9 10

April

May 14 15

June

July

August 19 20 21

September

October 24 25

November

December 29 30 31